BEARS
DON'T CRY!

Emma Chichester Clark

First published in hardback in the United Kingdom
by HarperCollins *Children's Books* in 2022
First published in paperback in 2023

HarperCollins *Children's Books* is a division of
HarperCollins*Publishers* Ltd
1 London Bridge Street, London SE1 9GF

www.harpercollins.co.uk

HarperCollins*Publishers*
Macken House, 39/40 Mayor Street Upper
Dublin 1, D01 C9W8, Ireland

1 3 5 7 9 10 8 6 4 2

ISBN 978-0-00-849187-1

Emma Chichester Clark asserts the moral right to be identified
as the author and illustrator of the work.

A CIP catalogue record for this title is available from the
British Library.

Printed and bound in China

THIS BOOK BELONGS TO

George was no ordinary bear.
He lived in the summerhouse in a garden
belonging to his dear friend, Clementine,
and her mother. Clementine had
taught George to read.

Clementine and her mother **loved** George.

He was very good company and
always helpful around the house.

He was never happier . . .

than when
he felt . . .

he was being useful.

Each day, when Clementine went to school and her mother went to work, George would settle down in the back garden to read.

Clementine's mother left him with **wonderful** books she'd borrowed from the library.

One day, George finished his book early. He knew it would be a long time before Clementine and her mother came home, so he decided to be very brave and go to the library all by himself.

Why have I never done this before? he wondered, as he strolled along the sunny street.

Well, it really was a lovely sunny day. But the sight of
a large, wild brown bear ambling along the road
had sparked a panic all over town. So when George
arrived at the library, he found that it was closed.

"Bother!" said George.

On the other side of the street there was a shop selling newspapers.

They'll know what time the library opens, thought George.

But suddenly, and mysteriously, the newspaper shop was closed too.

"Bother!" said George. "Just missed it."

Next, George went to the cake shop to ask about the library, but it said CLOSED on the door.

"I'm sure it was open a moment ago," sighed George.
Things happen quickly here, he thought.
I suppose that's what towns are like.

The market was buzzing with people, so George headed over there.

If only **someone** *would stop for a second.*

But before he had even said
"Hello" or "Excuse me",
everyone had vanished.

The market
was empty . . .

or was it?

George bent down to look.

"AIEEE!"

"HELP!"
shrieked the stallholders.

George leaped back in alarm. "OH!" he cried.

"Oh, no . . ." cried George.   "I can't stop . . .

SAVE ME!" cried George.

"H-E-L-P!"

And then there was something no one
had expected to see!

A flying bear . . .

a galumphing great bear, flying across the square.

The crowd gaped and gasped. And then . . .

they laughed.

Mamma mia!

Oh, my heavenly days!
Now I've seen
everything!

Oh, poor George!
Everything had happened so quickly.

What a disaster . . .

But why was everyone
laughing? He wondered.
They weren't laughing at
him . . . were they?

And the library book . . . George fished it out
of the water. It was ruined, of course.

"How clumsy I am," he sighed.
"How hopeless and clumsy."

He climbed out of
he pool sadly. But just
then, Clementine ran
out from the crowd.

When George saw her,
he **burst** into tears.

The crowd went quiet.
Then somebody whispered,

"Bears don't cry, do they?"

Clementine looked at poor George and then she looked at the crowd. Then she stood up and spoke to them.

"This is my dear friend, George," she said.
"He may be big – but you have hurt his feelings."

Everyone looked at each other. They didn't think a big bear would cry. But that's exactly what had happened.

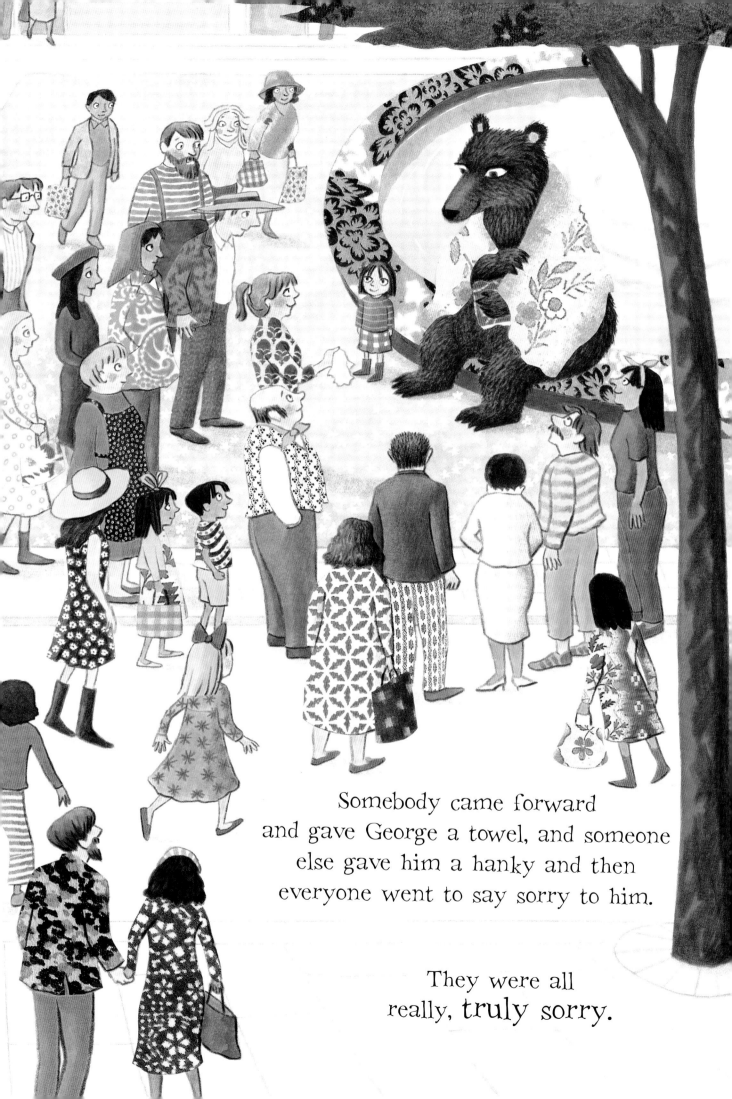

Somebody came forward
and gave George a towel, and someone
else gave him a hanky and then
everyone went to say sorry to him.

They were all
really, **truly sorry.**

The librarian brought George a new library book.
She said, "Don't worry about the old one.
I'll take it home and dry it out."

And then someone in the crowd said,
"Bears don't **read**, do they?"

So, George stood up, nervously.
He opened the book and began reading.

And that was another thing no one
had expected to see – but it was a
wonderful thing. They all stood
quietly, listening to George until
the book was finished.

The next day, the librarian came to tea with Clementine and her mother and George.

There was just one anxious moment . . .

when everyone held their breath . . .

and feared disaster . . .

. . . but it all
turned out perfectly,
in the end.